The Velveteen Rabbit

by Margery Williams

Illustrated by
Katherine Wilson

ideals children's books.

Nashville, Tennessee

ISBN-13: 978-0-8249-5530-4
ISBN-10: 0-8249-5530-7
Published by Ideals Children's Books
An imprint of Ideals Publications
A Guideposts Company
Nashville, Tennessee
www.idealsbooks.com

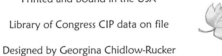

Color separations by Precision Color Graphics, Franklin, Wisconsin
Printed and bound in the USA

Library of Congress CIP data on file

Designed by Georgina Chidlow-Rucker

Worz_Jan13_3

There was once a velveteen rabbit, and in the beginning he was really splendid. On Christmas morning, when he sat wedged in the top of the Boy's stocking with a sprig of holly between his paws, the effect was charming.

For at least two hours the Boy loved him, and then Aunts and Uncles came to dinner, and in the excitement of looking at all the new presents the Velveteen Rabbit was forgotten.

For a long time he lived in the toy cupboard or on the nursery floor, and no one thought very much about him. He was naturally shy, and being only made of velveteen, some of the more expensive toys quite snubbed him. The mechanical toys were very superior and looked down upon everyone else; they were full of modern ideas and pretended they were real.

The Rabbit could not claim to be a model of anything, for he didn't know that real rabbits existed; he thought they were all stuffed

with sawdust like himself. Between them all, the poor little
Rabbit was made to feel very insignificant and
commonplace; and the only person who was kind
to him at all was the Skin Horse.

he Skin Horse had lived longer in the nursery than any of the others. He was so old that his brown coat was bald in patches and showed the seams underneath.

"What is REAL?" asked the Rabbit one day, when they were lying side by side. "Does it mean having things that buzz inside you and a stick-out handle?"

"Real isn't how you are made," said the Skin Horse. "When a child loves you for a long, long time, not just to play with, but REALLY loves you, then you become Real."

"Does it happen all at once, like being wound up," he asked, "or bit by bit?"

"It doesn't happen all at once," said the Skin Horse. "You become. It takes a long time. By the time you are Real, most of your hair has been loved off, and your eyes drop out and you get loose in the joints and very shabby. But these things don't matter, because once you are Real you can't be ugly, except to people who don't understand."

There was a person called Nana who ruled the nursery. Sometimes she went swooping about and hustled the toys away in cupboards.

One evening, when the Boy was going to bed, he couldn't find the china dog that always slept with him. Nana was in a hurry, and it was too much trouble to hunt for china dogs at bedtime, so she simply looked about her and made a swoop.

"Here," she said, "take your old Bunny!" And she dragged the Rabbit out by one ear and put him into the Boy's arms.

That night, and for many nights after, the Velveteen Rabbit slept in the Boy's bed. At first he found it uncomfortable, for the Boy hugged him very tight, and sometimes he rolled over on him. But very soon he grew to like it, for the Boy would talk to him and make nice tunnels for him under the bedclothes that he said were like the burrows the real rabbits lived in. And when the Boy

dropped off to sleep, the Rabbit would snuggle down
close under his little warm chin and dream,
with the Boy's hands clasped close
round him all night long.

And so time went on, and the little Rabbit was very happy—so happy that he never noticed how his beautiful velveteen fur was getting shabbier and shabbier, and his tail coming unsewn, and all the pink rubbed off his nose where the Boy had kissed him.

Spring came, and wherever the Boy went the Rabbit went too. He had rides in the wheelbarrow and picnics on the grass. And once, when the Boy was called away suddenly to go out to tea, the Rabbit was left out on the lawn until long after dusk, and Nana had to come and look for him because the Boy couldn't go to sleep unless he was there. He was wet through with dew and quite earthy from diving into the burrows the Boy had made for him in the flower bed, and Nana grumbled as she rubbed him off with a corner of her apron.

"You must have your old Bunny!" she said. "Fancy all that fuss for a toy!"

The Boy sat up in bed and stretched out his hands.

"Give me my Bunny!" he said. "You mustn't say that. He isn't a toy. He's REAL!"

When the little Rabbit heard that, he was happy, for he knew that what the Skin Horse had said was true at last. He was Real. The Boy himself had said it.

That was a wonderful Summer!

Near the house where they lived there was a wood, and in the long June evenings the Boy liked to go there to play. He took the Velveteen Rabbit with him, and before he wandered off to pick flowers, or play among the trees, he always made the Rabbit a little nest somewhere among the ferns where he would be quite cozy. One evening, while the Rabbit was lying there alone, watching the ants that ran to and fro between his velvet paws in the grass, he saw two strange beings creep out of the tall ferns near him.

They were rabbits like himself, but quite furry and brand-new. They must have been very well made, for their seams didn't show at all, and they changed shape in a queer way when they moved; one minute they were long and thin and the next minute fat and bunchy, instead of always staying the same

like he did. Their feet padded softly on the ground, and they crept quite close to him, twitching their noses.

They stared at him, and the little Rabbit stared back. And all the time their noses twitched.

W hy don't you get up and play with us?" one of them asked.

"I don't feel like it," said the Rabbit.

"Ho!" said the furry rabbit. "It's easy as anything." And he gave a big hop sideways and stood on his hind legs.

"I don't believe you can!" he said.

"I can!" said the little Rabbit. "I can jump higher than anything!" He meant when the Boy threw him, but of course he didn't want to say so.

"Can you hop on your hind legs?" asked the furry rabbit.

That was a dreadful question, for the Velveteen Rabbit had no hind legs at all! The back of him was made in all one piece, like a pincushion. He sat still in the ferns, and hoped that the other rabbits wouldn't notice.

"I don't want to!" he said again.

But the wild rabbits have very sharp eyes. And this one stretched out his neck and looked.

"He hasn't got any hind legs!" he called out. "Fancy a rabbit without any hind legs!" And he began to laugh.

"I have!" cried the little Rabbit. "I have got hind legs! I am sitting on them!"

"Then stretch them out and show me, like this!" said the wild rabbit. And he began to whirl round and dance.

"I don't like dancing," he said. "I'd rather sit still!"

But all the while he was longing to dance, and he felt he would give anything in the world to be able to jump about like these rabbits did.

The strange rabbit stopped dancing, and came quite close. He came so close this time that his long whiskers brushed the Velveteen Rabbit's ear, and then he wrinkled his nose suddenly and flattened his ears and jumped backwards.

"He doesn't smell right!" he exclaimed. "He isn't a rabbit at all! He isn't real!"

"I am Real!" said the little Rabbit. "I am Real! The Boy said so!" And he nearly began to cry.

Just then there was a sound of footsteps, and the Boy ran past near them, and with a stamp of feet and a flash of white tails the two strange rabbits disappeared.

"Come back and play with me!" called the little Rabbit. "Oh, do come back! I know I am Real!"

But there was no answer, only the little ants ran to and fro, and the ferns swayed gently where the two strangers had passed. The Velveteen Rabbit was all alone.

"Oh, dear!" he thought. "Why did they run away like that? Why couldn't they stop and talk to me?"

For a long time he lay very still, watching the ferns, and hoping that the rabbits would come back. But they never returned, and presently the sun sank lower and the little white moths fluttered out, and the Boy came and carried him home.

Weeks passed, and the little Rabbit grew very old and shabby, but the boy loved him just as much. He loved him so hard that he loved all his whiskers off, and the pink lining to his ears turned grey, and his brown spots faded. He even began to lose his shape, and he scarcely looked like a rabbit any more, except to the Boy. And then, one day, the Boy was ill.

His face grew very flushed, and his little body was so hot that it burned the Rabbit when he held him close. Strange people came and went in the nursery, and a light burned all night. And through it all the little Velveteen Rabbit lay there, hidden from sight under the bedclothes; and he never stirred, for he was afraid that if they found him someone might take him away.

It was a long weary time, for the Boy was too ill to play, and the little Rabbit found it rather dull with nothing to do all day long. But he snuggled down patiently, and looked forward to the time when the Boy should be well again, and they would go out in the garden amongst the flowers and butterflies and play splendid games in the raspberry thicket like they used to. All sorts of delightful things he planned, and while the Boy lay half asleep he crept up close to the pillow and whispered them in his ear.

And presently the fever turned, and the Boy got better. He was able to sit up in bed and look at picture books, while the little Rabbit cuddled close at his side. And one day, they let him get up and dress.

It was a bright, sunny morning, and the windows stood wide open. They had carried the Boy out on the balcony, wrapped in a shawl, and the little Rabbit lay tangled up among the bedclothes, thinking.

The Boy was going to the seaside tomorrow. Everything was arranged, and now it only remained to carry out the doctor's orders. They talked about it all, while the little Rabbit lay under the bedclothes, with just his head peeping out, and listened. The room was to be disinfected, and all the books and toys that the boy had played with in bed must be burnt.

"Hurrah!" thought the little Rabbit. "Tomorrow we shall go to the seaside!"

Just then Nana caught sight of him.

"How about this old Bunny?" she asked.

"That?" said the doctor. "Why, it's a mass of scarlet fever germs! Burn it at once. Get him a new one. He mustn't have that anymore!"

And so the little Rabbit was put into a sack with the old picture books and a lot of rubbish, and carried out to the end of the garden behind the tool house. That was a fine place to make a bonfire, only the gardener was too busy just then to attend to it. He had the potatoes to dig and the green peas to gather, but next morning he promised to come quite early and burn the whole lot.

That night the Boy slept in a different bedroom, and he had a new bunny to sleep with him. It was a splendid bunny, all white plush with real glass eyes, but the Boy was too excited to care very much about it. For tomorrow he was going to the seaside, and that in itself was such a wonderful thing that he could think of nothing else.

And while the Boy was asleep, dreaming of the seaside, the little Rabbit lay among the old picture books in the corner behind the tool house, and he felt very lonely. The sack had been left untied, and so by wriggling a bit he was able to get his head through the opening and look out.

He was shivering a little, for by this time his coat had worn so thin and threadbare from hugging that it was no longer any protection to him. He thought of those long, sunlit hours in the garden—how happy they were—and a great sadness overcame him. Of what use was it to be loved and lose one's beauty and become Real if it all ended like this? And a tear, a real tear, trickled down his little, shabby velvet nose and fell to the ground.

And then a strange thing happened. For where the tear had fallen, a flower grew out of the ground—a mysterious flower, not at all like any that grew in the

garden. It was so beautiful that the little Rabbit forgot
to cry, and just lay there watching it. And
presently the blossom opened, and out of
it there stepped a fairy.

She was quite the loveliest fairy in the whole world. Her dress was of pearl and dewdrops, and there were flowers round her neck and in her hair, and her face

was like the most perfect flower of all. And she came close to the little Rabbit and gathered him up in her arms and kissed him on his velveteen nose that was all damp from crying.

"Little Rabbit," she said, "don't you know who I am?"

The Rabbit looked up at her, and it seemed to him that he had seen her face before, but he couldn't think where.

"I am the nursery Fairy," she said. "I take care of all the playthings that the children have loved. When they are old and worn out and the children don't need them anymore, then I come and take them away with me and turn them into Real."

"Wasn't I Real before?" asked the little Rabbit.

"You were Real to the Boy," the Fairy said, "because he loved you. Now you shall be Real to everyone."

$\mathcal{A}$nd she held the little Rabbit close in her arms and flew with him into the wood.

It was light now, for the moon had risen. All the forest was beautiful, and the fronds of the ferns shone like frosted silver. In the open glade between the tree trunks, the wild rabbits danced with their shadows on the velvet grass; but when they saw the Fairy, they all stopped dancing and stood round in a ring to stare at her.

"I've brought you a new playfellow," the Fairy said. "You must be very kind to him and teach him all he needs

to know in Rabbitland, for he is going to live with you
forever and ever!"

And she kissed the little Rabbit again and put him
down on the grass.

"Run and play, little Rabbit!" she said.

But the little Rabbit sat quite still for a moment and never moved. For when he saw all the wild rabbits dancing around him, he suddenly remembered about his hind legs; and he didn't want them to see that he was made all in one piece. And he might have sat there a long time, too shy to move, if just then something hadn't tickled his nose, and before he thought what he was doing he lifted his hind toe to scratch it.

And he found that he actually had hind legs! Instead of dingy velveteen he had brown fur, soft and shiny, his ears twitched by themselves, and his whiskers were so long that they brushed the grass. He gave one leap and the joy of using those hind legs was so great that he went springing about the turf on them, jumping sideways and whirling round as the others did, and he grew so excited that when at last he did stop to look for the Fairy she had gone.

He was a Real Rabbit at last, at home with the other rabbits.

$\mathcal{A}$utumn passed, and winter, and the spring. When the days grew warm and sunny, the Boy went out to play in the wood behind the house. And while he was playing, two rabbits crept out from the ferns. One of them had strange markings under his fur, as though long ago he had been spotted, and the spots still showed through. And about his little soft nose and his round black eyes there was something familiar, so that the Boy thought to himself:

"Why, he looks just like my old Bunny that was lost when I had scarlet fever!"

But he never knew that it really was his own Bunny, come back to look at the child who had first helped him to be Real.